World Space Week is October 4–10.

Hubb

Can you find these hidden objects?

flyswatter
slice of pie
lizard
toothbrush
pencil
needle
ice-cream cone

comb
crown
open book
sailboat
bell
banana

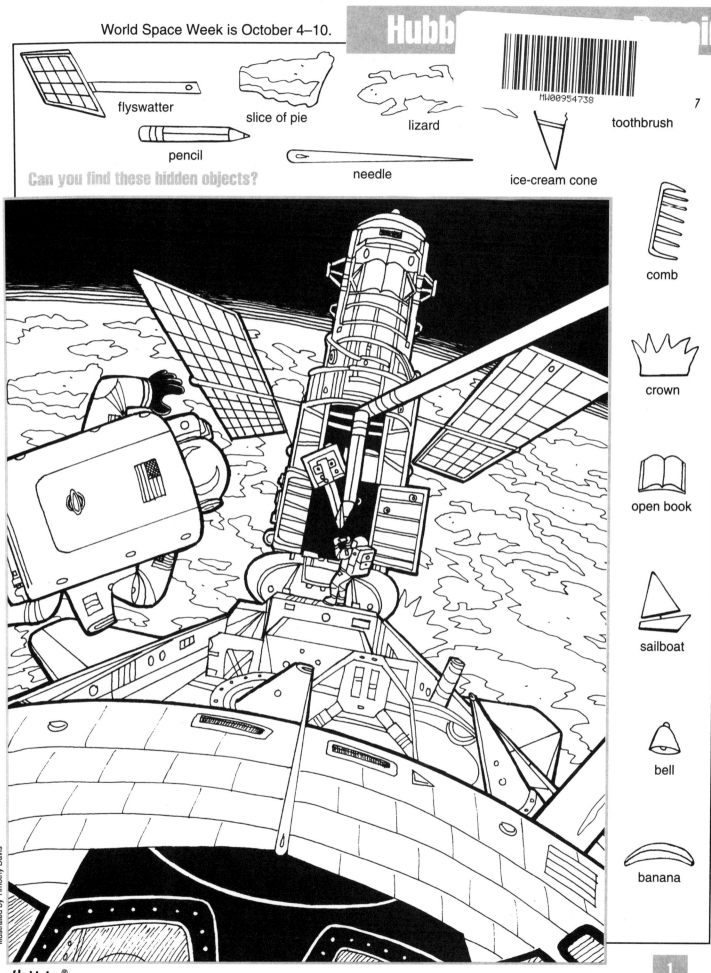

Illustrated by Timothy Davis

Highlights®

crayon

tack

banana

slice of pie

shovel

feather

pushpin

Can you find these hidden objects?

golf club

magic wand

mitten

candle

spoon

Illustrated by Charles Jordan

Highlights®

In 1806—200 years ago—the grandson of President Thomas Jefferson was the first child born in the White House.

pencil

loaf of bread

worm

slice of bread

needle

funnel

pennant

artist's brush

carrot

toothbrush

heart

spool of thread

closed book

Can you find these hidden objects?

banana

umbrella

slice of pie

nail

flag   candle

Illustrated by Sally Springer

Highlights®

3

banana

leaf

cupcake

slice of pizza

teacup

clothespin

Can you find these hidden objects?

pickax

fishhook

rolling pin

wishbone

nail

pennant

Illustrated by R. Michael Palan

Highlights®

Summer begins on June 21.

Rise and Shine

fishhook

lollipop

cane

horseshoe

mallet

toothbrush

spoon

witch's hat

golf club

Can you find these hidden objects?

fork

crescent moon

teacup

handbell

bat

SUMMER CAMP

Illustrated by Arieh Zeldich

Highlights®

5

Flying High

November is Aviation History Month.

cupcake

mushroom

candle

slice of pie

safety pin

toothbrush

Illustrated by Charles Jordan

Can you find these hidden objects?

ring

radish

pushpin

slice of cake

needle

dish

Highlights®

September is National Chicken Month.

Here, Chick, Chick

Can you find these hidden objects?

goose · fish · bat · toothbrush · hat · mouse · glove · heart · bell · tweezers · coat hanger · sailboat

Mouse Birthday

slice of pizza

ballpoint pen

crescent moon

key

trowel

hammer

Can you find these hidden objects?

musical note

teacup

golf club

pennant

Santa's hat

boot

ice-cream cone

Highlights®

National Salad Week is July 25–31.

Salad Factory

balloon

mug

needle

paper clip

ring

sock

tack

barbell

drinking straw

toothbrush

mushroom

Can you find these hidden objects?

slice of cake

crown

slice of bread

snail

fishhook

ice-cream bar

crescent moon

paper airplane

mallet

worm

Illustrated by Olivia Cole

Highlights®

Sledding Snowman

bell

slice of cake

scrub brush

flashlight

golf club

pushpin

Can you find these hidden objects?

banana

slice of pie

heart

ice-cream bar

tube of paint

nail

Illustrated by Charles Jordan

10

Highlights®

Benjamin Franklin, statesman, printer, and inventor, was born on January 17, 1760—300 years ago.

Can you find these hidden objects?

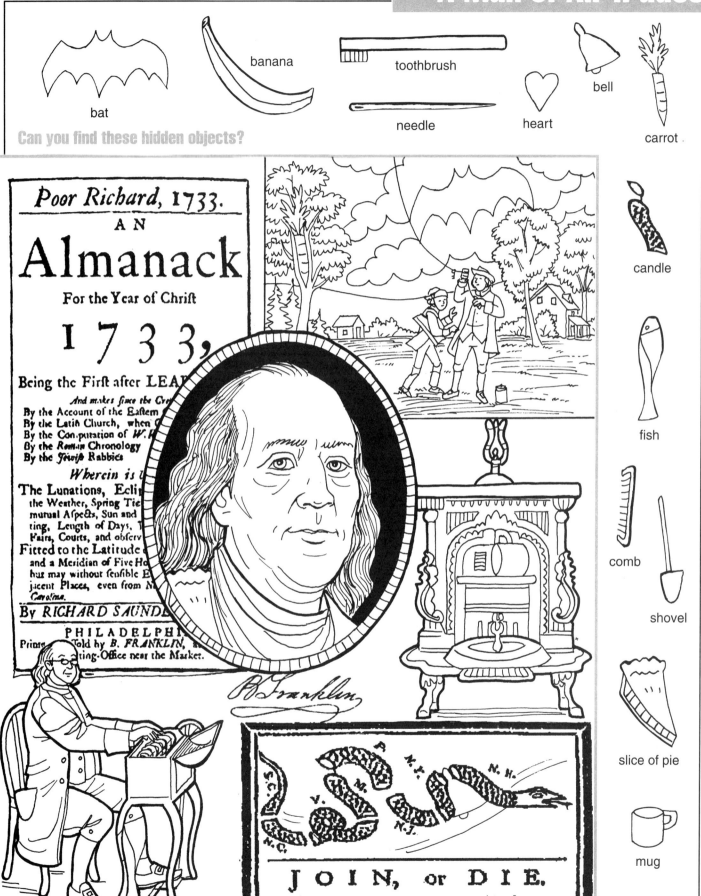

bat

banana

toothbrush

needle

heart

bell

carrot

candle

fish

comb

shovel

slice of pie

mug

In February, the 2006 Winter Olympics will feature this game that originated in Scotland during the 16th century.

toothbrush

crescent moon

pencil

snail

penguin

flag

Illustrated by Maurie Jo Manning

Can you find these hidden objects?

bell

piece of candy

light bulb

feather

ladle

umbrella

fork

Highlights®

Jungle Expedition

eyeglasses

bow tie

canoe

slice of pie

fish

hot dog

scissors

Can you find these hidden objects?

hairbrush

comb

glove

crayon

pliers

FIELD GUIDE TO THE JUNGLE

FALLS

SWAMP

carrot

nail

mallet

fishhook

coat hanger

drinking straw

Can you find these hidden objects?

toothbrush

golf club

wishbone

bat

teacup

bear's head

saucepan

needle

The railroad engineer, celebrated in "The Ballad of Casey Jones," was born on March 14, 1864—142 years ago.

boot

can

ice-cream cone

tack

muffin

top hat

Can you find these hidden objects?

doughnut

ladder

rowboat

needle

crescent moon

envelope

Come all you rounders if you want to hear
A story 'bout a brave engineer,
Casey Jones was the rounder's name
'Twas on the Illinois Central that he won his fame.

Highlights®

15

Block Party

September 24 is National Good Neighbor Day.

banana

slice of bread

apple

envelope

chicken

Can you find these hidden objects?

feather

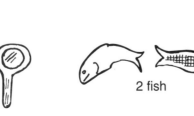
hand mirror

2 fish

heart

ice-cream cone

fork

leaf

acorn

frog

cane

duck

mushroom

carrot

slice of pizza

bat

2 birds

rabbit

Illustrated by Larry DiFiori

Highlights®

17

First Forward Pass

clothespin

paintbrush

closed book

eagle's head

necktie

Can you find these hidden objects?

pitcher

mouse

hammer

cupcake

cap

ladle

teacup

Illustrated by Susan Detwiler

18

Highlights®

Mama Possum and Family

eyeglasses

kite

wishbone

mitten

wristwatch

ring

needle

safety pin

snake

candle

porcupine

Can you find these hidden objects?

spoon

sailboat

pear

crescent moon

teacup

feather

the POSSUMS

glove

feather

paper clip

banana

pennant

candle

BEEHIVE LOOKOUT

WARNING! BEARS AT PLAY

HONEY HONEY

Illustrated by David Helton

Can you find these hidden objects?

paintbrush

spoon

golf club

artist's brush

spatula

tack

slice of pie

snail

20

Highlights®

Games for All

boot

ring

teacup

paper clip

Can you find these hidden objects?

fish

saw

eyeglasses

banana

bell

button

pear

pencil

ice-cream cone

Illustrated by Timothy Davis

Highlights®

21

October is National Cookie Month.

tack

candle

peanut

ladle

slice of pie

nail

mitten

Can you find these hidden objects?

toothbrush

pennant

slice of bread

ring

needle

worm

Illustrated by R. Michael Palan

22

Highlights®

July 20 is Special Olympics Day.

toothbrush

slipper   hammer   mushroom   shoe   canoe   mug   musical note   bell   slice of pizza

boot

ladle

bird

sailboat

slice of bread

crescent moon

pitcher

Can you find these hidden objects?

Illustrated by Linda Weller

Highlights®

July is National Recreation and Parks Month.

needle

pencil

baseball cap

tweezers

candle

Can you find these hidden objects?

fork

boot

dog bone

clothespin

fish

chicken

bell

cane

toothbrush

Illustrated by George Wildman

Highlights®

April 9–15 is National Garden Week.

celery

hoe

crown

slice of pie

clothespin

spoon

nail

slipper

hammer

fish

pear

sailboat

ladder

candle

golf club

Can you find these hidden objects?

Illustrated by Linda Weller

Highlights®

25

Morning Ride

adhesive bandage

banana

caterpillar

flashlight

sock

Can you find these hidden objects?

bell

envelope

lollipop

moth

scissors

spoon

dustpan

drinking straw

mushroom

knitted hat

lock

heart

needle

kite

nail

fishhook

ice-cream cone

slice of watermelon

artist's brush

pencil

Illustrated by Ellen Appleby

October 13 is World Egg Day.

teacup

crescent moon

toothbrush

spoon

needle

Can you find these hidden objects?

envelope

coat hanger

eyeglasses

crown

shoe

pencil

mallet

lollipop

Illustrated by R. Michael Palan

Flower's Bed

mallet

screw

needle

artist's brush

flag

candle

mop

wedge of lemon

Can you find these hidden objects?

ladle

heart

musical note

ring

spoon

glove

Illustrated by Larry Daste

Highlights®

Friendly Scarecrow

March 20, the first day of spring, is National Agriculture Day.

teddy bear

pennant

toothbrush

golf club

teacup

Can you find these hidden objects?

sailboat

mitten

loaf of bread

bell

ice-cream cone

saucepan

shoe

artist's brush

slice of pizza

mushroom

2 fish

Illustrated by Maggie Swanson

Highlights®

pushpin

feather

needle

toothbrush

paw print

pencil

mushroom

rabbit

shoe

heart

ice-cream cone

Can you find these hidden objects?

sailboat

seal

cinnamon bun

goose

pine tree

Illustrated by Susan T. Hall

The Great Backyard Bird Count is in February.

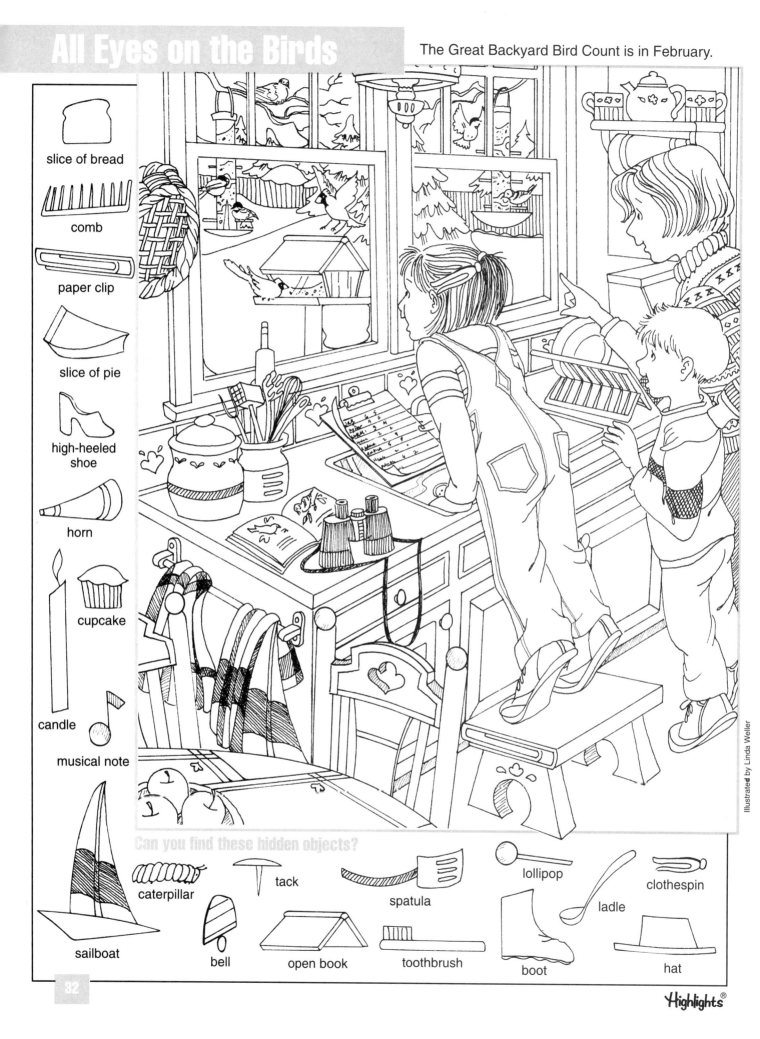

slice of bread

comb

paper clip

slice of pie

high-heeled shoe

horn

cupcake

candle

musical note

sailboat

Can you find these hidden objects?

caterpillar

tack

spatula

lollipop

ladle

clothespin

bell

open book

toothbrush

boot

hat

Illustrated by Linda Weller

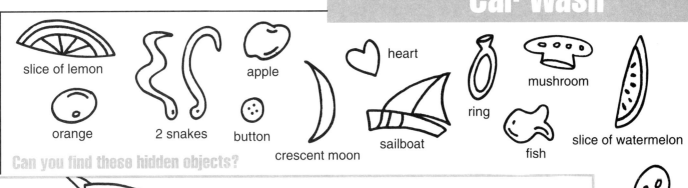

slice of lemon

apple

heart

mushroom

orange

2 snakes

button

crescent moon

sailboat

ring

fish

slice of watermelon

Can you find these hidden objects?

ghost

envelope

peanut

slice of pizza

tennis ball

arrow

mug

Illustrated by Jane Ramsey

Highlights®

pair of shorts

artist's palette

crown

ring

pinwheel

slice of pizza

sock

fried egg

football

Can you find these hidden objects?

needle

bowl

toothbrush

ice-cream cone

Illustrated by George Wildman

Highlights ®

slice of orange

envelope

toothbrush

pencil

hammer

closed book

glove

golf club

tack

spool of thread

baseball bat

ice-cream bar

elephant

fish

snake

saw

candle

domino

arrow

Can you find these hidden objects?

DANCE STUDIO

PET SHOP

Illustrated by Maggie Swanson

Highlights®

pushpin

candle

feather

grapes

slice of bread

ballpoint pen

Can you find these hidden objects?

toothbrush

golf club

shovel

snow shovel

banana

radish

fishhook

ladle

open book

key

bell

nail

magnifying glass

ring

ice-cream bar

cane

apple core

mitten

Illustrated by Charles Jordan

New Shoes for Smoky

July 9–15 is National Farrier's Week.

sailboat

mushroom

slice of bread

bell

pitcher

Can you find these hidden objects?

fish

mallet

crayon

spoon

telescope

teacup

flashlight

canoe

sock

candle

Illustrated by Linda Weller

Highlights®

▼ Page 1

▼ Page 2

▼ Page 3

▼ Page 4

Answers

▼ Page 5

▼ Page 6

▼ Page 7

▼ Page 8

Highlights®

▼Page 9

▼Page 10

▼Page 11

▼Page 12

Answers

Highlights®

▼Pages 16–17

▼Page 18

▼Page 19

the Possums

Answers

▼ Page 20

▼ Page 21

▼ Page 22

▼ Page 23

▼ **Page 24**

▼ **Page 25**

▼ **Pages 26–27**

Answers

▼ Page 28

▼ Page 29

▼ Page 30

▼ Page 31

Highlights®

▼Page 32

▼Page 33

▼Page 34

▼Page 35

Answers

▼ Pages 36–37

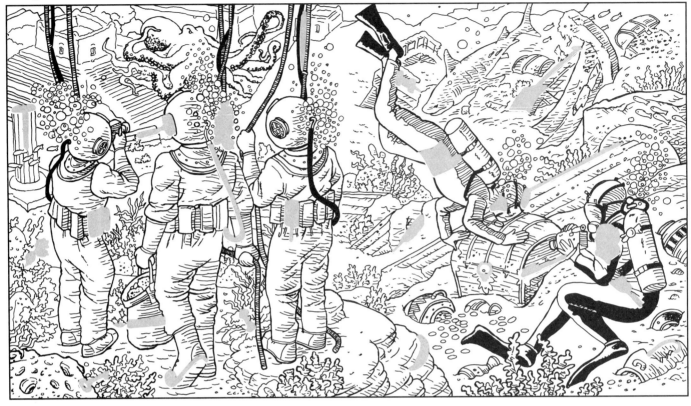

▼ Page 38

▼ Cover

Highlights®